D0098641

DISNEY
Aladdin

The Magic of Agrabah

The Mariner:

Once, in a far-off land . . .

Lindy: Baba, why are you telling us a story again?

The Mariner: It could be that I feel you children would benefit from a story about not judging by appearances. About appreciating what lies below the surface . . .

Barro: It's because we complained about how old and rickety our boat is, isn't it?

The Mariner: If you are patient, and listen, all will become clear. Besides, it is high past time I told you the story of Aladdin and his magic lamp. I think you will find it enlightening . . .

Lindy: I think you're just trying to distract us from the boat conversation.

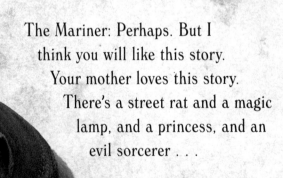

The Mariner: Perhaps. But I think you will like this story. Your mother loves this story. There's a street rat and a magic lamp, and a princess, and an evil sorcerer . . .

Barro: Is there a monkey?

The Mariner: You know, I think there is a monkey. Now . . .
Once upon a time, there was a far-off kingdom. It rested among the
shifting desert sands, caressed by the silver moon at night and the
golden sun in the day. It was a mysterious land, with a mysterious
name . . . Agrabah! ~

Lindy: Never heard of it.

The Mariner: Of course you haven't, that's why I'm telling you about it
now. No more interruptions. Once again . . . Agrabah!

The Mariner: In this kingdom lived a humble orphan, who made his home on the streets of this vast and wealthy city. Although he was penniless, he had a heart of gold, and never stole more than what he needed to survive. What he stole, he often gave away to those even more unfortunate, for his kind heart could not bear to see others suffering.

His name was Aladdin.

~

Lindy: Was he handsome, Baba?

The Mariner: What difference does that make? He was kind, and generous, and—

Lindy: Make him handsome!

Barro: And fast and nimble, too. He has to be those things, doesn't he, Baba?

The Mariner: Fine. Although I can't help but feel you children are missing the point of this tale.

Barro: And he should have a monkey!

The Mariner: He did have a monkey.

Aladdin's best and only friend was Abu the quick-fingered monkey, who had been with him for as long as he could remember. Together, the two made a life for themselves, fending off the city guards, sneaking food from the vendors in the marketplace, and doing all that they could to ensure their survival just one more day. It was a hard life, but it was theirs.

Aladdin had big, big dreams. One day, he swore, he would be more than a boy from the streets. He would be . . . somebody. Sometimes he would tell the vendors at the marketplace about his grand ambitions, but they only laughed at him. "A street rat will never be anything more than a street rat," they told him.

Aladdin didn't listen.

Lindy: What about the princess?

The Mariner: The princess comes in later.

Lindy: Princesses always come in later. That means they only ever get half a story. Why can't she come in now?

The Mariner: . . . You know what? You have a point, my dear.

As Aladdin made his home in forgotten alleyways and corners, he—and all the other citizens of Agrabah—could only look on in awe at the great palace that lay at the heart of their city.

But to Princess Jasmine, only daughter of Agrabah's great Sultan, the palace was nothing but a gilded cage. Every day she planned a way to sneak out to explore. And every day she was caught just before she reached the outside world.

Still, the thought of giving up never once crossed her mind. Princess Jasmine had never truly seen the kingdom beyond the palace walls, never walked among its people as one of them. And this was what she desired most, out of anything else in the world. For you see, Jasmine had dreams, too. Although no woman had ever ruled the kingdom, she wanted to succeed her father as the Sultan of Agrabah. She thought that if she could only prove to her father that she was ready for the task, he would grant her wish.

Her father, however, dismissed this idea out of hand. His plans were to marry Jasmine to a suitable prince, and once she was safely married, her husband would rule Agrabah. End of discussion. ~

Lindy: But why?

The Mariner: The Sultan had his reasons, my darling.
Misguided or not, he was trying to do what he
thought was best.

The Mariner: The Sultan was not a cruel or callous man—just afraid. Many years before, his beloved wife had been killed by thieves. Ever since that terrible day, he had become more and more protective of his only daughter. And he had a thousand years of tradition to teach him how to do just that. Of course, this only made Jasmine more desperate to prove that she did not need protection.

In the palace, Jasmine's only true friends were her pet tiger, Raja, and Dalia, her handmaid. And it was Dalia who eventually helped Jasmine sneak out by smuggling her beyond the palace walls. Jasmine would pretend to be a handmaid and return within a few hours so that she would not be missed.

Soon, Jasmine was walking the streets of Agrabah in her clever disguise. And what a sight greeted her! At first, she was overwhelmed and delighted by the sights and the sounds, but slowly, steadily, she began to notice that things did not quite seem right. Her mother had once told her that a kingdom was only as happy as its unhappiest subject, and she knew her mother would be heartbroken by the state of things now. Agrabah was a peaceful city, and had not been at war for many, many years, but armed guards seemed to stand at every street corner. She noticed citizens—even children—were going hungry.

This reality was one that Jasmine could not bear. Her heart aching, she took a piece of bread from a market stall and handed it to a pair of hungry children. She didn't think of it as stealing, but of course, it was, and the vendor was not amused, nor swayed by Jasmine's protests that she would return with the money to pay. He called for the guards, and before she knew it, Jasmine was cornered, inches away from having to reveal herself and her deception.
And this is where our story truly begins.

Who should step forward to help her . . . but Aladdin!

Barro: Aw, I knew he would. The story would be too short if she got caught right away.

The Mariner: Aladdin had seen the city guards at work, and he knew how unforgiving they could be. He may have had no idea who the girl in trouble truly was, of course, but it was plain to see that she hadn't meant any harm. He also knew exactly what to do to distract everyone long enough for him and the girl to get away.

Jasmine was wearing a bracelet, the one piece of finery that she'd brought with her on her adventure. Stepping in, Aladdin slipped the bracelet from her wrist, and handed it to the stall's owner. "Here you are, my good man," he said smoothly. "Take it as payment for the bread." The vendor grunted and put the bracelet on his own wrist. Jasmine was about to protest, but then watched in surprise as Aladdin cleverly took it back before the man had any idea what was happening.

Aladdin took Jasmine by the hand and began walking swiftly away with her. Jasmine understood and followed silently. They were half a street away, nearly lost in the crowd, when the vendor realized their

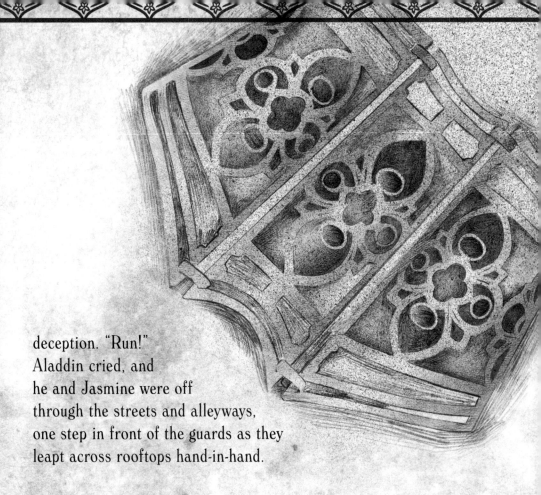

deception. "Run!"
Aladdin cried, and
he and Jasmine were off
through the streets and alleyways,
one step in front of the guards as they
leapt across rooftops hand-in-hand.

Jasmine followed Aladdin's every move, shocked and delighted at
herself—after so many years living protected inside the palace, safe
as a chick inside its shell, she finally felt as though she were living!
They ran and ran and ran, but despite their best efforts, found
themselves cornered on a parapet, surrounded by guards.

"Do you trust me?" Aladdin asked, holding his hand out to her, and
Jasmine nodded just as Aladdin handed her a long pole and sent her
sailing over the parapet, leaping over a gap between the roofs that she
would have thought impossible to clear. She laughed, giddy at her own
boldness as he followed her.

Eventually they managed to slip away from the guards, still laughing
at how much fun they were having, despite the danger they were in.

Aladdin knew that they wouldn't be safe if they stayed on the street. He took Jasmine by the hand and led her to his secret hideaway, an abandoned room high above the city, with beautiful views of the palace.

"I can't believe I did that!" Jasmine exclaimed, a smile of pure delight seeming to light her from within. "And I don't even know your name!"

"Aladdin," he replied, already beginning to like this girl with the lovely smile and the melodious laugh, who wasn't afraid to leap across rooftops with him hand-in-hand. "And you?"

"Dalia," Jasmine told him. She couldn't reveal who she truly was, after all. But she, too, already liked this kind and daring boy who had helped her.

Aladdin looked her over, then said, "You're from the palace, aren't you?" Jasmine was shocked—how had he known?

Aladdin took out the bracelet she had worn earlier. He knew that it was too fine for a commoner to wear. Together with her perfume, her finer-than-average clothes—he guessed at her identity. He figured that she must be handmaid to the princess herself.

Lindy: Ooh, so close!

The Mariner: And yet so far.

~

Still, strangers though they were, Aladdin and Jasmine recognized
something in one another. A similarity, a bond. Although to some eyes they
seemed as far apart as they could be, each felt trapped in their roles, in
their lives. It was as if they could see it in each other, and it brought them
closer. Each shared a little of themselves, Aladdin telling Jasmine of his life
on the street, Jasmine commiserating with the feeling of being stuck in a
place you weren't meant to be.

For Aladdin at least, something began to bloom.

Barro: Wait, Baba—

The Mariner: Yes, Barro?

Barro: You said there was a magic lamp in this story. And an evil sorcerer.

The Mariner: Telling you that they'll come in later won't help, will it?

Barro: Nope!

The Mariner: Very well then.

~

Aladdin and Jasmine weren't the only two who struggled with their places in life, of course. Within the palace dwelled Jafar, the Sultan's most trusted advisor. And although perhaps once he had been a man with noble intentions, time and a hunger for power had twisted and corrupted him. He may have appeared to serve the Sultan, but every day he conspired and plotted, searching for a way to overtake the throne.

Over the years, Jafar worked his way closer to the throne. With his parrot Iago as his spy, there was nothing that happened in the entire palace that he did not know about. But this was not enough. It was never enough. For Jasmine did not trust Jafar, and no matter what he did, he could not win the Princess over to his side. Jafar also knew that as soon as Jasmine was married, her husband would be next in line as Sultan, pushing Jafar further from the throne. Jafar had to claim the throne before that happened, no matter what.

Jafar had one hope. By studying ancient stories and scrolls he had learned of a magic lamp that could grant your heart's desires. But it lay in the depths of The Cave of Wonders, in the furthest, most impassable reaches of the desert, an enchanted place that only one could enter. One whose worth lay far within—a "diamond in the rough." And Jafar had no idea where he might find such a one.

~

Lindy: It's Aladdin, isn't it?

The Mariner: Come now, answering that would spoil the tale.

Lindy: It's definitely Aladdin.

Jasmine and Aladdin were talking together, still only just getting to know one another, when the two of them heard the peal of trumpets across the city. A procession was forming at the docks. A royal procession. It was another prince coming to court the Sultan's daughter.

Jasmine knew at once that she had to return to the palace before she was missed, or else she and Dalia would be in very deep trouble. Aladdin offered to escort her back, and remembering how easy it had been to misstep, Jasmine readily accepted his help.

They strolled back together, but as they drew near the palace gates, Jasmine realized that she had almost forgotten to get her bracelet back. "Do you have it?" she asked Aladdin.

"Of course," said Aladdin, patting his pocket.

But the bracelet was gone.

Aladdin's surprise was plain on his face, but Jasmine misread his expression as guilt. Her disappointment and betrayal was clear— maybe her father had been right. She trusted too easily. "That bracelet was my mother's," she said. "I should have known."

Aladdin opened his mouth to protest, but before he could utter a word, Jasmine ran from him, back toward the palace, disappearing into the crowd. Aladdin watched her go, feeling a longing and sadness in his heart. He was stunned at how their meeting had soured, and disheartened at the thought that this girl he thought might understand him now believed him to be a common swindler.

~

Lindy: Why didn't he go after her, Baba? Explain?

The Mariner: Oh, he tried.

~

By the time Aladdin was able to pull himself together, the royal procession was in full swing. Prince Anders of Skånland and his entourage had arrived, and they were standing between Aladdin and the palace gates. Carriages, drummers, soldiers, ah, it was an impressive sight. But this royal procession wasn't too careful about where it was going, and Aladdin noticed a pair of children about to be trampled under the hooves of a guard's horse.

Not only was no one taking Jasmine seriously, but they were also severely mistaken if they thought a clown such as Anders was a worthy suitor.

Jasmine sighed, thinking of having to attend more evenings of tiresome social events before she figured out a way to send this suitor packing like all the others.

~

Lindy: I love this princess.

In the Sultan's inner sanctum that evening, Jafar and the Sultan argued. Jafar had long been pressing the Sultan to declare war on the neighboring kingdom of Shirabad.

With Shirabad conquered, Jafar reasoned, Agrabah could turn its sights to the next country, and the next. A war would keep the Sultan busy, and perhaps give Jafar even more opportunities to reach new heights of power. With his magic staff, he tried to hypnotize the Sultan into agreeing to his plan.

But just as Jafar had begun to make progress, Jasmine interrupted, demanding to know why they were speaking of war on Shirabad. It was their oldest ally, she pointed out, and her mother's homeland. Jafar's spell broken, the Sultan immediately reassured her that there would be no war. "But I'm not getting any younger, my dear," he pointed out. "We must find you a husband, and we're running out of kingdoms . . ."

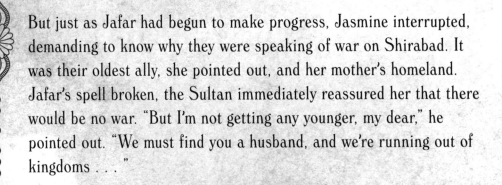

"Raja would make a better ruler than the princes I've met so far!" Jasmine protested. "And what foreign prince could care for our people as I do? Why can't I—"

"No woman has been Sultan in the thousand-year history of our kingdom," her father interrupted.

"And you have no experience," Jafar added.

"I've studied," said Jasmine. "I've read books. I care for our people—"

"We each have a role to play, Princess," Jafar replied, dismissing her once more. "Leave the serious matters to us."

~

Barro: I really don't like that guy.

Lindy: Me either.

~

"Leave the serious matters to us, they said," Jasmine told Dalia in her room that night. "If I leave matters to them, we will end up in an unnecessary war!"

"Well, you could always marry the rich, handsome prince," Dalia teased. "Or would you prefer the thief from the marketplace?" Jasmine had, of course, relayed every detail of her adventure to Dalia, who was intrigued by her story.

Just then, Jasmine heard a noise at the door. She walked to the corridor, and was surprised to find herself face-to-face with the very man that she and Dalia had just been discussing.

"What are you doing here?" Jasmine asked.

It hadn't been easy to sneak into the palace, and Aladdin had been hoping for a little warmer of a welcome. But he was glad to see her, even if it didn't seem that "Dalia" was as happy to see him.

"I'm returning your bracelet," Aladdin explained, and Jasmine looked down to see that her mother's bracelet was already back on her wrist. She hadn't even noticed Aladdin move to do it. She put her fingers to it, touched by the kind gesture, but also amazed at Aladdin's appearance in the palace.

"And you had to break into the palace to do it?" she said, perhaps more sharply than she intended. Still, he had entered without permission.

"How else was I going to see the princess's personal handmaid?" Aladdin grinned, and despite herself, Jasmine was just a little bit charmed at his recklessness. "I'm sorry about that, by the way. Abu stole it when I wasn't looking. I hope I won't get you in trouble . . . with the princess, I mean."

"No, but you'll be in trouble if anyone sees you," Jasmine said, shaking her head. "You should go. Now."

Aladdin could tell she was uncomfortable, although he couldn't quite tell why. She was worried for him, and maybe still a little angry about the bracelet. He agreed to leave, but added, "If you won't come to see me, I'll find my way back here," and plucked a hairpin from Jasmine's hair. "Tomorrow, when the moon is by the minaret, I will meet you in the garden to return this." He unpinned it, giving her one half. Jasmine took it, unable to help but smile at his audaciousness. "I promise."

Aladdin left, and he might as well have been walking on air as he made his way out of the palace, Abu perched on his shoulder. He couldn't believe that he had just made it into the most impregnable building in Agrabah, with no one the wiser!

With this smug thought, he turned a corner and suddenly found himself in the middle of a band of guards, none of whom looked very happy to see him. Then, for Aladdin, everything went black.

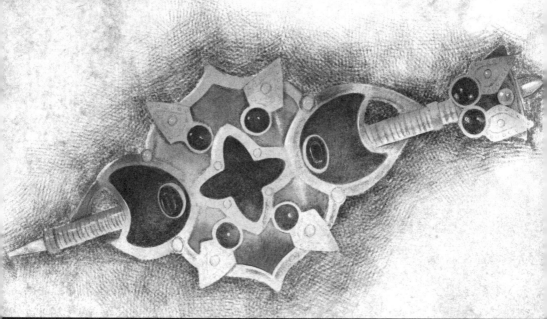

When Aladdin next awoke, he was at an unfamiliar oasis, surrounded by endless sand on all sides. A couple of palace guards were nearby, watering their camels, and he could see Abu's head poking out of one of the saddlebags. There was no sign of any civilization; he had clearly traveled far while he was unconscious.

Sitting beside him was an unfamiliar man, who had obviously been waiting for him to wake up.

~

Barro: Jafar!

The Mariner: Correct, my boy.

~

Aladdin didn't know this, but Jafar had been watching him since he entered the palace grounds by scaling a wall. He'd seen Aladdin return Jasmine's bracelet and knew that this kind of nobility in a street rat was a rare thing. At last, perhaps, he had found his "diamond in the rough." There was only one way to find out.

Jafar began by explaining that the handmaid that Aladdin had come to see was actually the princess Jasmine herself. "The princess?"

Aladdin stammered. "I have a date with the princess?"

"Hardly," Jafar replied. "It amuses her to meet commoners, that is all." He told Aladdin that it was the princess's hobby to go in disguise among the peasantry, but that it was just that, a hobby. Aladdin had no real chance with her.

Jafar lied, of course, but it was easy enough for Aladdin to believe. After all, he'd never met a princess before. Uncertain, he listened as Jafar told him that he too had once been a mere commoner. But with cleverness and patience, Jafar had begun to accumulate wealth and power. He now worked alongside the Sultan, in the palace. And he was willing to extend a helping hand to Aladdin; in exchange for a "small" favor, he would make Aladdin a rich man.

"All that you must do is enter a nearby cave," Jafar said. "Inside you will find a simple oil lamp. Pick it up and return it to me." In exchange, Jafar promised, he would make Aladdin wealthy beyond his wildest imagination.

Perhaps even wealthy enough to impress a princess.

In the light of the moon, Jasmine sat in the palace gardens, waiting in vain for Aladdin to arrive. He had promised her, hadn't he? She touched the half of the hairpin he had left her, trying to convince herself that he hadn't deceived her. Why would he have risked his life and snuck into the palace to return her bracelet if he hadn't been serious? She gave the moon one last look as it dipped behind the minaret, then sighed and returned inside.

Unknown to her, Aladdin was gazing up at the same moon as he and Jafar crossed the desert on camelback, eventually arriving at the mouth of The Cave of Wonders. It was not a welcoming place. Half-buried in sand, the opening was the gaping mouth of an enormous lion, teeth bared in a roar. It seemed poised to swallow Aladdin whole. He shuddered, looking at Abu, who seemed just as apprehensive.

"No one has been worthy enough to enter in many years," said Jafar. "But I think you are the one to succeed where others have failed." Aladdin was not so sure. And yet . . .

What did he have to lose? And if Jafar was telling the truth, then everything in his life would change. Perhaps he would finally be more than a street rat. Perhaps even worthy of a princess. He touched the hairpin in his pocket, remembering Jasmine's smile when he had promised to meet her again.

Jafar warned him that he would see seemingly endless treasures within the cave. He would be tempted beyond imagining. "But remember," Jafar said gravely, "take nothing but the lamp."

Aladdin nodded his assent. Cautiously, he approached the cave, watching in alarm as the lion's eyes began to glow. A whisper, seeming to emanate from the desert itself, reached his ears.

Only one may enter here
One whose worth lies far within
A diamond in the rough

Perhaps, Aladdin thought belatedly, this was not such a good idea. Before he could change his mind, however, the sands at the cave mouth swirled around his ankles, dragging him toward the entrance. In a matter of seconds, he was swallowed whole.

Blinking sand out of his eyes, Aladdin realized that he was on a stairway, with nowhere to go but down, deeper into The Cave of Wonders. It took him many minutes, but Aladdin was agile and strong, and reached the bottom without difficulty, Abu clinging nervously to his neck. Only then did he realize how the cave had gotten its name.

Diamonds, sapphires, rubies, gold . . . a sea of treasures stretched as far as the eye could see. Aladdin's jaw dropped as he took it all in. Jafar had been right. Even in his wildest dreams, he never could have pictured such riches. Remembering Jafar's repeated admonishments, he tried to keep his hands to himself. But Abu was not so cautious. His clever monkey fingers reached out toward a sapphire, but a warning rumble from the cave alerted Aladdin to Abu's faltering willpower. Clearly, the cave could tell when it was about to be plundered.

"Abu!" Aladdin scolded, picking him up and setting him on his shoulder. He would have to keep a closer eye on his friend. "Remember, we can't touch anything. Let's find the lamp."

They wandered for a time among the heaps of treasure, dazzled. Even with the warnings, Aladdin felt tempted—every corner they turned revealed new and greater opulence. He was so overwhelmed that he reached out, unthinking, toward one particularly lovely gemstone, but pulled his hand back sharply. Too sharply. He stumbled, and fell back.

To his surprise, he fell on something soft. To his greater surprise, it was a carpet, hovering just above the ground. Could it be? A magic carpet? He'd heard stories of such things. He bent to examine it more closely, and the carpet moved, then floated upright, gesturing with its tassels to one of its corners. It was pinned under a heavy treasure chest. With care, Aladdin moved the chest, and the carpet floated free. Then it moved swiftly forward, wrapping Aladdin in a hug.

It wasn't just magic—it was alive. And very friendly.

Of course, it was only one of many strange things that had happened to Aladdin that night. He was prepared to accept this further strangeness. "So, Carpet," Aladdin asked. "You wouldn't happen to have seen a lamp around here?" After all, there was no one else around to ask.

The carpet nodded, and gestured upward. On a rocky outcropping far above their heads lay an ordinary-looking brass oil lamp.

Admonishing Abu to stay put and not touch anything, Aladdin began to climb up. As he approached, the treasures grew larger and more lustrous, the temptation ever-increasing. But Aladdin had his eyes on his true goal now, and was able to ignore those tantalizing distractions.

Abu, however . . . well, he had a little less self-control. At the same moment Aladdin finally reached for the lamp, Abu's greed got the better of him, and he grabbed a giant glimmering gemstone.

There was an outraged roar from the cave. The rules had been broken. The wall beside Aladdin began to split and crumble. Lava gushed forth, beginning to fill the cave and turn the golden treasures around them into a moving molten trap.

The magic carpet grabbed Abu and soared toward Aladdin, flying with frantic speed, clearly wanting to repay Aladdin's earlier kindness. Holding the lamp, Aladdin leapt onto the carpet, just as the ceiling above him began to collapse. The cave's roaring grew louder—deafening, and it was all Aladdin could do to hang on as the magic carpet flew toward the entrance as quickly as a magic carpet could go.

~

The Mariner: Are you two alright? The story is getting a little scary now.

Barro: I'm fine, Baba!

Lindy: Yes, keep going!

~

Rivers of molten gold flowed beneath them, bubbling and fountaining all around. Several times Aladdin thought they were done for, but the carpet dodged the dangers expertly until the mouth of the cave was in sight.

There, Aladdin could see Jafar, holding a torch aloft, waiting for his return. Waiting for the lamp.

They were nearly out. They had nearly escaped. But mere feet from the exit, their luck ran out. A falling rock struck the magic carpet, sending Aladdin flying forward with Abu clutching his shoulder. Aladdin managed to leap onto a crumbling ledge just below where Jafar was waiting.

"Did you get it?" Jafar shouted over the sound of the cave-in.

"Yes!" Aladdin replied, raising the lamp in one hand. The ledge beneath him began to collapse, and with his free hand he clung to the rocks at Jafar's feet, looking up desperately as Abu clung to him.

"Grab onto me!" said Jafar, bending down, but Aladdin's other hand was still holding the lamp. "Give me the lamp and I'll pull you up!"

Aladdin didn't hesitate. He held the lamp up toward Jafar, who snatched it up, sticking it into a satchel. Then, ignoring Aladdin's outstretched hand, he began to walk away. "Wait!" Aladdin cried, unable to believe the betrayal.

~

Lindy: How dare he!

The Mariner: Abu felt the same way.

~

Furious, Abu leapt from Aladdin's back, chasing after Jafar and pounced to attack him. He scratched and bit, beating at Jafar's face to try to force him to turn back.

~

Barro: Good monkey.

~

But Jafar shook him off. With a final roar, the cave collapsed, and Jafar walked off alone into the night, leaving Aladdin and Abu to perish.

But Aladdin didn't perish.

He was back inside the cave, although it was nearly unrecognizable now. No more gold and jewels—only rubble and cooling dark lava. The carpet had caught him and Abu before they were dashed against the rocks, cushioning their fall. They were alive. But as Aladdin looked around, despairing, he could see that there was no way out. They were trapped.

Sensing the defeat in Aladdin and trying to find something to cheer his best friend, Abu slyly produced the lamp, which he'd snatched from Jafar's satchel during his attack. "You're a cunning little monkey," he said to Abu, patting him affectionately. At least Jafar hadn't gotten what he wanted after all. But it was small comfort—they still had no way out of the buried cavern.

Aladdin peered around the cave for a while, seeking any sign of an exit, but no such luck. "You're sure there's no other way out?" he asked the carpet, which shook its tassels expressively and emphatically no. Aladdin sat down in defeat, gazing at the lamp in his hands.

"All that for this old thing?" he murmured, peering closer at an engraving on its side. Curious, he rubbed it, trying to clear away the dirt and get a better look. For a moment, nothing happened.

Suddenly, red smoke began pouring from the spout, swirling around Aladdin's feet, building into a great column, and forming into a giant, terrifying figure. An enormous pair of arms stretched from the haze, flames filling the cave as the Genie of the lamp appeared!

The Mariner: With a booming voice, huge sharp teeth, and horns six feet long—

Barro: Okay, okay, too scary now, Baba!

Lindy: Much too scary. Why can't the Genie be friendly?

The Mariner: He is friendly! I didn't say he wasn't friendly! I did tell you not to judge by appearances.

Barro: He should be less scary. And blue!

The Mariner: All right, as you wish . . .

~

Blue smoke poured out of the lamp's spout, forming into an enormous figure, and so on and so forth, and the Genie of the lamp appeared!

"Oh great one who commands me, and terrible one who commands me—" the Genie began to say in a booming voice, then looked down at Aladdin in surprise. He looked around, then back at Aladdin. "Wait a second," he said in a much more normal tone, "where's your boss?"

"My boss?" Aladdin was still staring at the Genie. Again, this was just one of many strange things that had happened to him today, each stranger than the last.

The Genie sighed. "I've been doing this a long time, kid. The guys who rub my lamp, they're usually already all over me, wanting money, power, an army large enough to conquer the world . . . You? You don't fit the profile. You're sure *you* rubbed my lamp? It's just you and me in here?"

Aladdin nodded, dumbstruck.

"Well then, that makes you my master," the Genie said. "You rubbed my lamp, so you get the Genie, the three wishes, the whole thing."

Something in Aladdin's eyes said that he still didn't believe him. The Genie sighed. It was time to give a little demonstration.

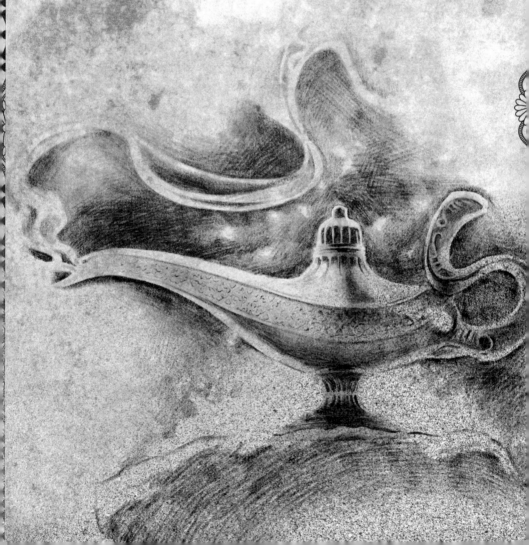

Aladdin was astounded. He'd heard stories of the Genie in the lamp—who hadn't heard the fairy tale? But this—this was the real thing. He could hardly believe it, but it didn't seem like he was dreaming. He decided to start with the basics.

"So … you can grant any wish?" he asked, still doubtful.

"Well, there are some limitations," the Genie admitted. "You have to hold the lamp and rub it, and say 'I wish.' Plus, I can't grant every wish. For example, you can't wish for more wishes, so don't try. And I can't make anyone fall in love with anyone else or bring people back from the dead. Other than that, the world is your oyster!"

Aladdin considered this carefully. Only three wishes. He had to make them count. His first wish should have been obvious—they needed to get out of the cave. But that seemed like a waste of an all-powerful cosmic being's powers. And a waste of a wish.

He picked up the lamp, looking up at the Genie, who seemed eager to leave the cave, and also didn't seem to be paying much attention. He slipped the lamp behind his back and casually passed it to Abu before saying, "Okay, Genie, I wish you to get us out of this cave."

"Finally!" the Genie exclaimed, and piled them onto the magic carpet, who was an old friend of his. He used his powers to rip through the ceiling of the cave, bursting out into the sunlight with the magic carpet just behind him. They made a bumpy landing on the sand outside the cave, the Genie gazing around with obvious pleasure and relief.

"The world is so big!" he sighed happily. "You forget that, locked in a lamp for a thousand years. That's the thing about being a Genie. Phenomenal cosmic power; itty-bitty living space!" He turned to Aladdin. "So, what are you going to wish for?"

Aladdin shook his head, the reality of the situation still not quite sinking in, the possibilities almost too vast to contemplate yet. "I don't know," he admitted. "What would you wish for?"

The Genie was taken aback. No one before had ever rubbed his lamp without a clear idea of what they wanted. And no one had ever asked him what he would wish for.

Still, he didn't even have to think about it. "I'd wish to be free," he said, for that was his greatest desire. "To not have to grant wishes anymore—to be my own master. To be human."

"You're all-powerful, aren't you?" Aladdin said, frowning. "Why don't you just free yourself?"

Genie laughed, but there was a little sadness in it. "That's not how it works, kid. I can't use my powers for myself. The only way I get free is if the owner of the lamp wishes me free. And that pretty much never happens."

Well, that seemed simple enough. "I'll wish you free," Aladdin said promptly, smiling. "I've got three wishes, don't I?"

"Two," Genie corrected automatically.

"Really? I thought I had to rub the lamp?" Aladdin's smile widened. Genie stared, then thought about it—it was true.

Aladdin hadn't rubbed the lamp when he wished them out of the cave. He hadn't even been holding it.

"All right, all right. Gonna have to keep my eye on you, I see," said Genie, folding his arms. "*Three* wishes, then."

"No more tricks, though, I promise," Aladdin said, crossing his heart with his finger. "And I really will use my third wish to set you free."

The Genie looked doubtful. He'd granted innumerable wishes, and he knew better than to get too excited. "Funny thing about wishes," he said. "The more you get, the more you want. Money, power . . . I've seen it drive people mad."

"That's not me," Aladdin promised. "But . . . there is one thing . . . " A look came into his eyes, a look that was all-too-familiar to the Genie.

"Uh-oh," he said, a smirk spreading across his face. "Who's the girl?"

"She's a princess," breathed Aladdin. The enormity of it struck him. Even when he thought she was a handmaid, she was already out of his league. Now that he knew she was a princess, the daughter of the Sultan, she was even more unattainable.

"Remember, I can't make anyone love anyone," the Genie warned, but Aladdin shook his head. That wasn't what he was getting at.

He thought about how she'd smiled at him when he handed her the hairpin. He could still feel its weight in his pocket. That smile—it was real. She felt something for him, that couldn't be a lie. Jafar had to be wrong about her. Of course, after his betrayal, Aladdin was sure he couldn't trust anything the man had said about anything.

"We had a connection," he said, feeling more sure of himself. "This princess . . . she's smart, and kind, and beautiful, but . . . she has to marry a prince." He sighed, feeling his heart sink. As himself, he had no chance. But a thought struck him suddenly. He had a magic lamp, three wishes—no one said he had to be himself anymore. He could just wish to be somebody else, couldn't he?

"Genie, can you make me a prince?" he asked.

The Genie held up a hand. "Okay, in the future, watch out how you wish. You don't want to know how fast a carelessly-worded wish can turn against you. You seem like a nice kid, so I won't get tricky on you . . . this time. Let's rephrase: You want to become a prince?"

Aladdin nodded eagerly.

"You're sure? If she already likes you—" The Genie looked dubious.

"No, I told you," Aladdin said, a little impatiently. "She has to marry a prince. If I'm a prince, then at least I'll have a chance with her."

"Okay, then, we gotta phrase it as an official wish. For those of us keeping count." The Genie looked stern. He wasn't about to allow himself to be tricked again.

Aladdin picked up the lamp, his heart pounding. This was really happening. "Genie," he said solemnly, "I wish to become a prince."

The Genie grinned and rubbed his hands together. "Let's get to work."

Meanwhile, back at the palace, Jasmine was attempting to have a heart-to-heart with her father. Agrabah's annual harvest festival was coming up, and for the past several years, it had been held on the palace grounds, limited to a certain caliber of guest. Jasmine was trying to convince her father that it was time to move the festival back outside, as it had once been.

"It's a nice thought, my dear," said the Sultan, his tone kind, "but the city is far too dangerous now."

"It isn't," Jasmine argued. "If you would go outside, you would see. And you'd see what Jafar is doing to the city—"

"And what would you know of the dangers of the city, Princess, venturing out as rarely as you do?" Jafar asked, walking in and deftly interrupting their conversation. "But, come to think of it, I did hear about a recent trip you took into the city . . . "

"What?" The Sultan looked at his daughter.

"Hakim saw her returning from the marketplace," Jafar said, gesturing to the head of his guards, a hulking man of few words. Hakim nodded, a little reluctantly—but it was true.

The Sultan turned to Jasmine. "I told you that you are not to leave the palace!" he said, incensed.

"Because that's what he wants!" Jasmine shot back, pointing at Jafar accusingly. "He wants to keep us prisoners in the palace so that he can rule in our place!" She turned to Hakim, pleading. "Hakim, tell my father that the city has changed. Tell him what

Jafar is doing, that his guards are the ones threatening our people, not criminals . . . "

Hakim remained silent, and the Sultan sighed. "I encouraged your interests as long as they did not put you in danger. But this is more than I can bear. You will stay inside the palace walls, do you understand?"

Before Jasmine could answer, Jafar bowed to the Sultan. "I will post more guards outside the princess's door at once, my Sultan," he said, and Jasmine glared at both of them before turning on her heels and storming out. She'd known that it had been a long shot, but she'd hoped that her father might believe her.

The Sultan sat stunned, watching her go, with Hakim close behind her. Perhaps he was wrong to discount his daughter's advice. He knew that she was wise beyond her years—she took after her mother in that way. Her mother . . .

The Sultan's thoughts turned melancholy. He only wanted to protect his daughter. It was possible, in his eagerness to keep her safe, that he had gone too far.

"She may be right, Jafar," he sighed. "We have become . . . less involved in the city's affairs. Too removed. Jasmine is an intelligent girl. Perhaps she could join us in our council meetings?"

But Jafar could not allow this. He could not control Jasmine like he could control her father—the possibility of her joining the council, shaving away even a little of his power, was unacceptable. His hard-won control would slip from him like sand through his fingers.

Jafar raised his staff. It glowed faintly with magical energy, and he stepped toward the Sultan, speaking in a smooth, low tone. "You must protect Jasmine and keep her in the palace," he said, invoking an enchantment to bend the Sultan's will to his. "You must find her a prince before she gets herself into trouble . . ."

The Sultan's features relaxed, slackened. He was hypnotized. "I must find her a prince," he repeated, slowly. "Never fear, sire," Jafar said smoothly. "I'm sure someone will turn up."

Just then, Hakim returned to the room, a look of surprise on his normally stony face. "A foreign delegation has entered the city, my Sultan," he said, and the Sultan and Jafar turned to look at him in confusion. No delegation was supposed to arrive that day—indeed, no other suitors aside from Prince Anders had been considered for some time.

And yet there was the sound of trumpets and drums from outside . . .

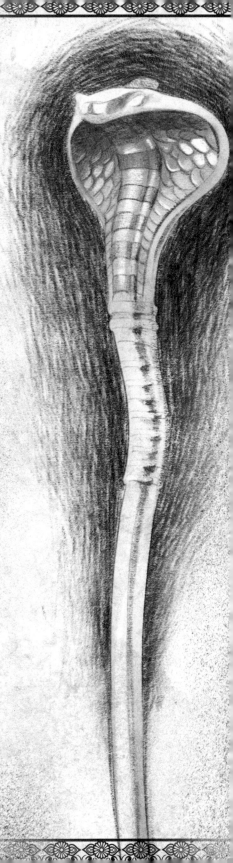

Aladdin had never been more terrified in his life.

For the Genie had done more than just make Aladdin look like a prince— he'd concocted a whole new identity, promising Aladdin that no one would recognize him as "Prince Ali of Ababwa." But riding on a float in the midst of a magical entourage, Aladdin couldn't help but begin to second-guess his wish. It was stupid, to think that he could fool so many people, to think that he could pass himself off as royalty. Who was he kidding?

But then the crowd began to cheer, looking up at him in awe. Aladdin raised a hand to wave, and people screamed in delight. Girls went weak in the knees. Aladdin blushed, then started to preen and play to the crowd as his confidence rose. He even saw a few people among them that he knew, but it was clear that—just as the Genie had promised— they could not see past his dazzling appearance. He was no longer Aladdin the street rat. He was Ali, a wealthy prince, coming to their city to court their princess as an equal.

With the Genie leading the way, disguised as a human, they soon reached the gates of the palace and were promptly ushered inside. No more sneaking around in the shadows, Aladdin thought. This was the life.

Before he realized it, he was standing in front of the Sultan. The Sultan. And just like that, his mind went blank. Stalling for time, he bowed, trying to think. Aladdin had lived his life on the street. He'd never met royalty. Except for Jasmine, and he'd been able to be himself then, but he hadn't known she was royalty. He didn't know how to think or act like a prince. What would Ali say?

Standing beside him, still in disguise as the prince's advisor, the Genie nudged him. Aladdin stood up.

"It's a pleasure to welcome you to Agrabah, Prince Ali," the Sultan said warmly.

"I'm uh, as pleasured as you are?" Aladdin replied, then cringed when he realized the words that had come out of his mouth. He waved his hands behind him, an awkward gesture. "I brought gifts. Um. Expensive gifts?" Servants brought forward silks, spices, and jewels. The Sultan looked delighted, and Jafar, standing nearby, looked suspicious. But to Aladdin's relief, the Genie's magic held even for him.

"And what do you hope to buy with these gifts?" came a familiar voice from behind him. Aladdin turned—it was Jasmine, with Dalia standing close behind her. His heart lifted to see her, then sank as their eyes met, with no recognition. Aladdin felt more and more awkward by the moment. It hadn't quite occurred to him that by disguising himself, he and Jasmine would have to start over.

"You?" he stammered. "I mean, um, a moment with you?"

~

Lindy: yikes. He was terrible at this, wasn't he, Baba?

Barro: Embarrassing.

The Mariner: Oh, my children. You have no idea.

~

Jasmine raised a critical eyebrow. "Are you suggesting I am for sale?" she inquired. As far as she could tell, this Prince Ali was the biggest fool that she'd yet met—and in her father's search for suitors, she'd met quite a few.

"No!" Aladdin fumbled, trying to recover and looking to the Genie for help. But the Genie was also a bit distracted—he had seen Dalia, and the pair were regarding one another with more than mild interest. Jasmine, however, had seen enough of "Ali." She tossed her hair over her shoulder and exited in disgust. Crestfallen, Aladdin watched her go, and Genie watched Dalia follow her. Both of them sighed, longingly.

"That's not what I meant," Aladdin mumbled.

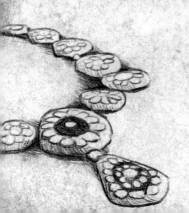

"Don't worry," said the Sultan, who had seen his daughter scorn many princes before and was unfazed. "You'll have a chance to speak again. Join us tonight, for the celebration of the harvest."

"This party is not a second chance," Genie told Aladdin later, as they settled into their royal quarters within the palace. "This is your last chance. I'm not going to lie, that was a disaster."

Aladdin put his head in his hands, mortified. He had expected life to be easier as a prince than a street rat. Pretending to be who he wasn't made him feel stiff and wrong, and the easy charm that he'd always had was just . . . not there.

"I think the Sultan liked me," he said, trying to find a silver lining.

"It's not the Sultan you're trying to marry," the Genie replied peevishly. "You need to show Jasmine that you're more than an awkward ball of nerves, and you need to do it tonight, or you'll blow it for good."

The Harvest Festival was an overwhelming crowd of Agrabah's most well-to-do, with fine clothes, fine music, and fine food and drink. Even with an all-powerful Genie at his side, Aladdin had never felt more out of place in his life.

"There's your girl," said the Genie, back in disguise as the prince's advisor, pointing across the crowd to where Jasmine and Dalia stood. "Go talk to her."

Aladdin steeled himself and began to walk over, but lost his nerve as he saw Prince Anders intercept her first. Anders seemed much more at ease than he was. And he was a real prince, not a pretender like Aladdin. He felt his meager remaining confidence drying up and blowing away.

"What can I even offer her?" he whispered as the Genie came to his side to find out what was keeping him from just crossing the gardens and talking to her. "I'm just a thief. Ali has jewels and servants and—"

"And you are not Ali," Genie replied. "I changed your outsides, kid, not your insides. You said you two had a connection, right? Was the connection with Ali, or was it with you? The real you? Now go talk to her, while her..."—Genie sighed, noticing Dalia walking away— "beautiful handmaid goes and gets some refreshments. Go!" And he pushed Aladdin forward.

~

Lindy: Ooooh, this should be good.

Jasmine had been watching Ali watching her, and so far she remained unimpressed, although she agreed with Dalia's whispered comments that there was something slightly endearing about him. Still, she was convinced he was yet another fool her father had dredged up, more interested in a military alliance with Agrabah than in knowing her as a person.

She almost didn't expect him to approach her again, and was somewhat surprised when he appeared in front of her, looking even more nervous than he had in the throne room earlier. "Hello," he said.

"Hello," she responded, and waited for him to say something else. He didn't, and she was almost ready to give up when he finally opened his mouth again.

"I'm sorry about earlier," he burst out. "That's not what I meant, I—I promise not to say anything else stupid."

"Does that mean you're going to say something intelligent?" Jasmine shot back. Ali looked so abashed that she felt a little sorry for him. There was something different about him—he was sweet, but unpolished and unsure. He seemed so skittish that she wondered for a moment if he'd ever been outside of his own country. The thought made her soften a bit.

"How about we just dance?" she said, offering him her hand. She led him out onto the dance floor, and they began to move to the music.

At first, they followed the steps of the people around them, elegant and proscribed, like the wheels of a clock. But as they danced together, Ali began to relax, breaking from the mold and losing some of his hesitation. He pulled her close, then spun her away, moving fluidly, clearly enjoying himself. To her surprise, Jasmine was enjoying herself, too. There was something familiar about his movements, his sudden confidence, though she couldn't put her finger on it.

From across the room, Jafar watched as well, frowning. The boy seemed familiar to him, too, though like Jasmine, he could not place the feeling. In any case, he was like no prince Jafar had ever seen, and he resolved to keep a close eye on this "Ali."

The music swelled, and Ali began to enjoy the spotlight. Jasmine began to think Prince Ali was like the other princes she had met after all.

She frowned deeply, turning away and quickly exiting the dance floor. Just another arrogant prince, she thought, ignoring his cry of "Wait!"

"No, he's still—" Aladdin replied, then froze.

"It is you. The boy from the market!" Jasmine was beaming triumphantly. "I knew it! Who is Prince Ali?"

"I am!" Aladdin replied quickly, covering frantically. "I . . . like to go among the people in disguise. Like someone else I know . . . ?"

"But you knew your way around the city so well . . . " Jasmine did not look convinced.

"I arrived early," Aladdin said, thinking on his feet. "I had to be sure about the alliance. And I had to sneak away . . . I mean, no one sees the real you when you're royalty. Surely, you understand." He gave her a meaningful look, and she began to look more certain, though he could still see doubt shadowing her face.

A moment hung in the air as they gazed at one another, then Jasmine shook her head. "I suppose we should get back," she said. "It's nearly morning."

Aladdin agreed reluctantly, though neither was quite ready for the night to end. "Tomorrow, Princess?" he asked, shyly returning her to her balcony. He was about to float away when Carpet nudged him forward, and the two shared a tender kiss.

~

Lindy: Aww!

Barro: Ewww.

"We should go," he said. "I mean, would you want to go? See those places? With . . . um, with me?"

Jasmine gave him a puzzled look. "How? Every door here is guarded."

"No one said we need to use a door," Aladdin replied, and stepped off the balcony. Jasmine gasped and rushed forward—only to see him standing on the magic carpet. "Do you trust me?" he asked, reaching his hand out to her.

Jasmine stared. She recognized the question. Then she took his hand.
~

Aladdin had shown Jasmine many beautiful sights that night, but none were more beautiful than Agrabah from above. Jasmine gazed down at her city, amazed at its loveliness. "They deserve a leader who knows how wonderful this place is," she said softly. "I wish I could show everyone that I can be that leader."

"What's stopping you?" Aladdin was curious.

Jasmine hesitated, then explained—haltingly at first, then with more passion. How she wanted to be Sultan, but how a woman had never been Sultan before. How much it bothered her to be passed over, when she felt so strongly that she could serve her people wisely and well.

To her surprise, Aladdin agreed, and Jasmine glanced at him. She knew this feeling. She was almost certain now. Almost . . .

"Look at that cute monkey down there," she said, pretending to look down, but really watching for his reaction. "Do you think that's Abu?"

Aladdin paced in his quarters. Somehow, he had ruined it again. He'd made a little progress, but spoiled it just as quickly. "If I just had a few more minutes with her," he murmured, then paused, looking at the Genie. "You have to help me get over there."

"Is that an official wish?" the Genie responded, unmoved.

"It's a favor. For a friend?"

The Genie looked even more unconvinced. "I don't do favors, kid. Or have friends."

Aladdin remembered how the Genie had gazed at Dalia. He knew that longing look. "You'll get to distract her handmaid."

That was all it took. "I'll meet you there," the Genie said, and vanished in a puff of blue smoke.

Moments later, the Genie was knocking on the princess's door, cloaked in his human disguise. When Dalia answered, she was charmed enough to agree to take a walk through the gardens with him, Jasmine delightedly shooing her out. At least Dalia could have a little fun, she thought sadly.

When she turned around, she let out a little cry, startled. Ali was standing on her balcony. "Don't be scared," he said quickly.

"I'm not, but maybe you should be," Jasmine replied coolly, gesturing to Raja, who was growling at the unexpected intruder. "Raja, don't eat the prince. I actually did want to see you, Prince Ali." She beckoned him inside, then gestured to a globe. "I was just looking for Ababwa on my map. I couldn't find it."

Aladdin paled—he hadn't thought of that. "Well, I mean," he murmured, trying to save face, "what good are maps anyway?"

"They're how I see the world," Jasmine replied, frowning.

Aladdin was surprised. "I would think a princess could go wherever she wished."

"Not this princess."

Aladdin remembered how easily Jasmine had been able to sympathize with him when they'd met, the feelings they'd shared of being trapped, and he had a sudden idea.

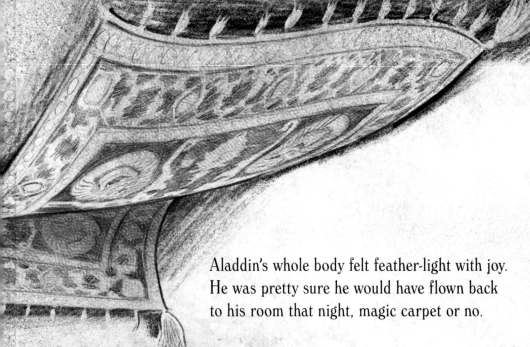

Aladdin's whole body felt feather-light with joy. He was pretty sure he would have flown back to his room that night, magic carpet or no.

"Good date?" the Genie asked when he got in.

"The best," Aladdin sighed, leaning back on the magic carpet, beaming as he remembered the events of the night. Then he sat up, frowning. "But Jasmine knew who I was! You said no one would know me!"

"I said no one would recognize you," Genie replied. "I didn't change what's inside. So . . . what did you tell her?"

. . .

In her chamber, Jasmine related the night's adventures to Dalia. "He told me he was really a prince," Jasmine said frowning. "And that he was only pretending to be a thief so that he could see the city."

"And you believed him?" Dalia's doubt reflected Jasmine's own.

"I think so?" Jasmine considered her answer. "He has a magic carpet, and that huge procession when he came to the palace . . ."

"You sure you don't just want to believe him? Because you can marry a prince, but not a thief?" Dalia asked gently.

"I'm . . . not sure," Jasmine admitted.

. . .

Aladdin concluded his version of the night's events to the Genie. "She believed that?" the Genie asked, incredulous. "You know that you're going to have to tell her the truth, right?"

"I am," Aladdin said, although the idea terrified him. And yet he knew that the Genie was right. "I'm going to tell her. Eventually."

~

Lindy: So did the Princess believe him or not?

The Mariner: Yes.

Barro: That's not an answer.

The Mariner: Sometimes we believe because we want to.

Lindy: That seems like a bad idea.

It was only a short while before sunrise, but Aladdin had no intention of sleeping. He was still too elated about how well his evening with Jasmine had gone. It would help, he thought, to take a walk around the grounds with Abu, to think a little more about how magical his time with Jasmine had been. And to think about how best to break the news that he was not really Prince Ali, just Aladdin.

He was so distracted that he almost didn't see Jafar's guards until they were right in front of him. Abu had time to jump from Aladdin's shoulder and conceal himself, but Aladdin only had enough time to mutter "Not again!" as they grabbed hold of him, and dragged him away.

Abu watched from the shadows, frozen with fear. He tried to follow, but quickly lost sight of the guards in the unfamiliar dark of the palace. Abu may have only been a monkey, but he was a clever monkey, and he knew that these guards were not good news. He had to help his friend.

He scampered back toward Prince Ali's royal quarters as quickly as he could, clambering up onto the bed and casting about frantically for the lamp. He tossed aside pillows and blankets, fine silks and turbans, finally finding it carelessly hidden under a large basket. He seized it, banging it on the floor, trying to open the lid, keening frantically, all to no avail. Finally, Abu blew into the spout, coughing as blue smoke boiled out in furious response. The Genie appeared, staring at Abu in annoyance as he frantically tried to signal that Aladdin was in trouble. But the Genie couldn't understand, finally shaking his head, bewildered.

"No monkeyshines tonight," the Genie said, clearly unamused. "Don't mess with my lamp." He retreated back into his confines of the lamp, and Abu, seeing no other choice, grabbed the lamp and ran.

Much like the last time he was taken by guards, Aladdin did not like the situation he was in. Not only was he tied to a chair at the top of one of the palace's tallest minarets, with the ocean crashing against the rocks a hundred feet or more below him, he was also face-to-face with the very last person he wanted to see: Jafar.

"Where is the lamp, Prince Ali?" Jafar asked pointedly.

Play dumb, thought Aladdin, and snapped back "What lamp?"

Jafar gestured to one of the guards standing nearby, who searched Aladdin's clothes. The guard found nothing, and Aladdin was relieved he'd left the lamp behind when he'd gone on his walk. "When the Sultan finds out about this—" Aladdin began, trying to summon a prince's righteous fury, but Jafar's eyes narrowed.

"Finds out what? That I've kidnapped Aladdin?"

Aladdin felt his heart leap into his throat. He remembered what the Genie had said—no one would recognize him. But that hadn't stopped Jasmine from knowing him. Jafar continued, "I had my suspicions, oh prince from a kingdom that doesn't exist, but when I saw you on a magic carpet, stolen from The Cave of Wonders, it all became clear."

Aladdin realized too late that he was in very real danger—Jafar was powerful, something he already knew well. "That's ridiculous," he protested, but weakly, and moved his wrists, trying to slip out of the ropes that bound him to the chair.

"Is it?" Jafar strolled to the edge of the balcony, almost casually, looking down at the water below. "I know one way to find out for certain. If I throw you off this balcony and you perish, I will be free of Prince Ali. If you survive, it can only be because you have the lamp. Either way—" he snapped his fingers, and the guards picked up the chair, carrying it toward the balcony—"I'll have my answer."

The guards heaved, and Aladdin fell. And fell and fell. The world seemed to freeze as he watched the water coming closer and closer, and then he was plunged into the roiling ocean.

Jafar watched the distant splash with satisfaction, then strolled away.

~

Barro: I really
don't like that
guy, Baba.

Abu clutched the lamp and watched in horror from the shadows, as Jafar had Aladdin tossed off the tower. He had finally found where Jafar had brought his best friend, but it seemed like he was too late. It was all the little monkey could do to hold still until Jafar left, knowing that if he was spotted, Jafar would steal the lamp.

He waited several agonizing seconds, then, when he was certain Jafar was gone, he scampered to the edge of the balcony and dropped the lamp over the side. He could only hope it was close enough to do some good.

Beneath the waves, Aladdin tried to break free. Then, a splash at the water's surface, and the lamp was suddenly, miraculously sinking through the water nearby.

Aladdin hit the bottom of the rocky shallows, the movement of the waves above rolling him back and forth like a piece of flotsam. He struggled against his constraints, using the weight of the chair to roll toward where the lamp landed only a few feet away. His air was rapidly running out, bubbles escaping his mouth as he fought for every inch.

It took a few tries before he was close enough to reach it. His hands were tied behind him, and he was forced to fumble blindly, until finally he felt the lamp's solid, reassuring shape in his hands. How long had he been down here? Two minutes? Five? He could barely keep his eyes open, but with the last of his strength and his breath, he rubbed the lamp.

The Genie roared out, prepared to scold Abu once more for touching his lamp—only to be stunned into silence when he saw Aladdin, unconscious, apparently at the bottom of the ocean.

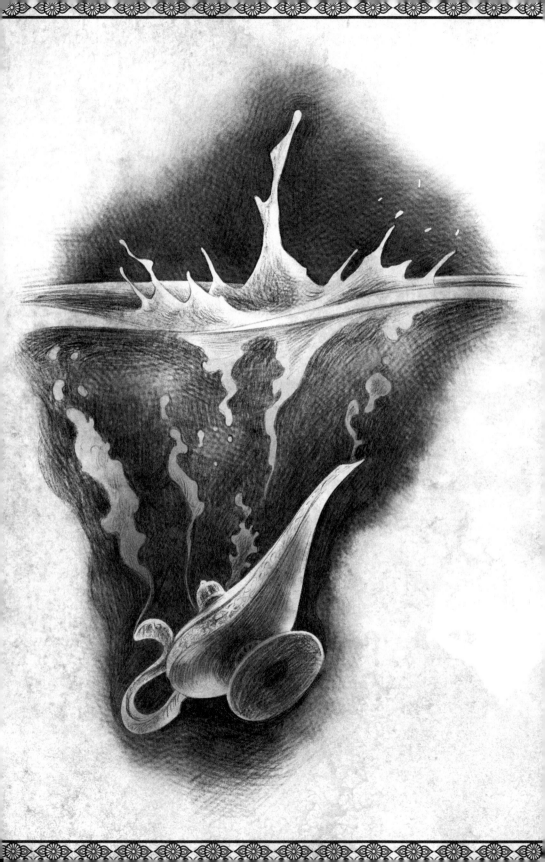

The Genie may not have known what had happened, but he understood the gravity of the situation at once. "Kid, I can't help you with this one," he said frantically, grabbing Aladdin by the shoulders and shaking him. "You have to wish."

Nothing. Aladdin floated, as silent and still as a . . .

~

Lindy: Don't say it!

Barro: Did he save him, Baba?

The Mariner: Well, the Genie had many masters over the centuries. None of them had been particularly kind. But something about Aladdin was different. The Genie could feel it. Maybe he didn't do favors. Maybe he didn't do friends. But all the same, he liked Aladdin. And so, he bent the rules. Just a little. Just this once.

~

"Come on, kid," the Genie muttered. "Say the words. 'I wish . . . ' Come on . . ." He leaned in, pretended to listen. Aladdin didn't move, didn't speak, but the Genie nodded as though the unconscious boy had spoken. "I heard it!" the Genie declared in desperation, then flew toward the surface, Aladdin in his arms.

He landed back inside the palace, setting Aladdin on the floor and bending over him to see if he was breathing. After a moment, Aladdin came to, coughing water and trembling. It had been a close call. Too close.

Still, the first words he spoke—when he was able to speak—were: "Thanks, Genie."

There was no time to lose, however. As soon as he was able to stand, Aladdin raced toward the throne room. He had to warn the Sultan of the snake in their midst.

And not a moment too soon. Before Aladdin had even sunk to the bottom of the sea, Jafar had awoken the Sultan to begin spinning a story of Prince Ali's treachery. Jasmine, alerted by the commotion, was trying to argue with him, but she was fighting a losing battle.

"I heard them, my Sultan," Jafar said, gravely. "Prince Ali and his advisor were speaking in hushed tones, planning to return to Agrabah with an invading army. They were never interested in the Princess—only conquest."

"It can't be," said the Sultan, dismayed. Jafar shook his head.

"His rooms are empty. It appears he has fled."

Jasmine broke in—she knew that Jafar could not be right. Prince Ali had been with her all night, not plotting an invasion. "He's lying, Baba!" she said desperately, but Jafar ignored her, pressing on.

"I have warned you, my Sultan," said Jafar. "Agrabah is vulnerable. We could be invaded at any moment . . ."

"That's not true!" Jasmine slammed a fist on the table, and her father looked at her, startled by her outburst. "I don't know what Jafar has done," she said, "but I know he is lying. Ali would not betray us like this." Of this she was certain. The boy who had shown her those wonderful places would never turn against her like that. And she knew that Jafar was up to something.

She was vindicated when Aladdin, still dripping wet and disheveled from his attempted assassination, pushed the doors open, striding inside with his eyes locked furiously on Jafar.

"Prince Ali!" cried the Sultan, relieved but also clearly confused by this turn of events.

"Your highness," said Aladdin, his voice clear and accusing, "your advisor is *not* who he says he is."

Jafar had been startled by Aladdin's reappearance, but not that startled. There was his answer—the boy had the lamp, after all. And if he had the lamp, Jafar could take it back. Subtly, he turned his magic staff towards the Sultan, dulling his mind.

"He had me abducted, tied to a chair—he tried to have me killed," Aladdin said, but the Sultan shook his head slowly, strangely.

"Terrible," he murmured, but it sounded suddenly as if he weren't really listening. "Just terrible."

"I'm lucky to be alive," Aladdin continued, confused by the Sultan's demeanor, watching him closely. He glanced at Jasmine, who was just as bewildered at her father's response.

"I don't know who to believe." The Sultan's voice sounded as if it were coming from far away.

"Believe Ali!" Jasmine said, leaning to look at her father in the eyes, but Jafar leaned in first, blocking her, keeping her at bay.

"My Sultan, you know I am telling you the truth," he said, in a low, hypnotic voice lulling the Sultan's senses. But Aladdin saw the glow of the staff, the way that Jafar held it steady in the Sultan's vision. As the Sultan began to repeat Jafar's words, Aladdin deftly snatched the staff from Jafar's hand.

Jafar was taken aback—he had been so careful, so subtle all these years, and no one had ever before noticed the staff. He found himself stunned as Aladdin whirled the staff over his head, then smashed it on the ground, where it shattered with a thunderous noise.

The Sultan blinked, seeming to come back to himself. "What?" he said, dazed, his expression beginning to clear. "What just happened?"

Aladdin held the smoking staff out toward the ruler of Agrabah, pointing toward Jafar with his other hand. "Jafar has been manipulating you, your majesty," he said, calmly. "Hypnotizing you with *this*."

Jasmine's eyes widened, and the Sultan looked between the staff and his most trusted advisor, unable to believe what he was hearing. And yet, the evidence was there, too overwhelming to dismiss.

Jafar, finding himself suddenly at a disadvantage, began a hasty retreat.

"Guards!" roared the Sultan, pointing to Jafar. "Arrest Jafar!"

Jafar glared at the guards—his guards until a moment ago—standing between him and the exit, and the Sultan, who had no idea what Jafar had sacrificed, what he'd done for Agrabah.

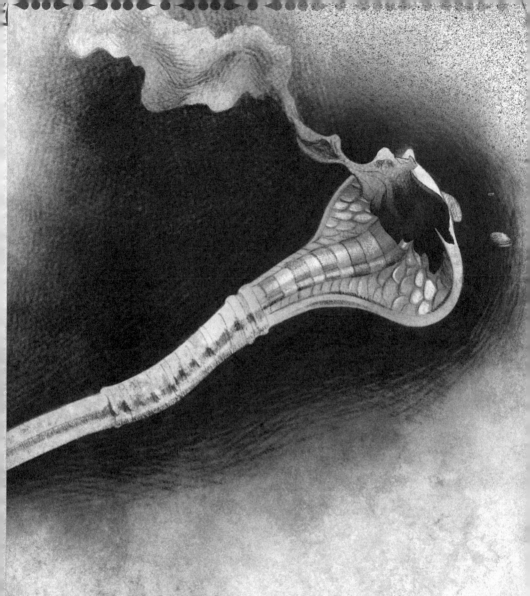

"I don't think so," he spat, and pulled a magical artifact from his robe. He held it aloft, and it surrounded him in a veil of smoke. In the blink of an eye, Jafar was gone.

"Find him!" the Sultan ordered, and the guards had no choice but to flee in pursuit.

~

Barro: Ugh, I hate it when the bad guy gets away.

"Prince Ali, I cannot apologize enough for how you were treated," said the Sultan, looking at Aladdin with concern. "You have done Agrabah a great service by revealing a venomous serpent in our midst. Your honesty and integrity will never again be questioned in this kingdom."

Aladdin smiled bashfully, although he was unable to help but feel a guilty pang at the Sultan's words. He was lying just by being there. The Sultan had even called him "Prince Ali." He had to come clean about his own deception, and quickly.

But the Sultan wasn't finished yet.

"A more noble and sincere young man has never before graced the halls of this palace," the ruler continued, beginning to beam proudly. "I would be proud to call you my son . . . if that were something that, say, anyone in this room would want . . . ?"

Aladdin's eyes widened, and he glanced over at Jasmine, who was blushing, looking back at him. She looked happy but torn, and Aladdin remembered how reluctant she had been to believe his princely cover story. He couldn't speak up now.

He grimaced in a way that the Sultan must have mistaken for a smile, for he clapped a hand on their shoulders, congratulating them both heartily.

. . .

"Congratulations!" the Genie echoed, as Aladdin sat in his chambers later that day, head in his hands, agonizing over the web of deception he'd created for himself.

"Now you can tell her the truth!" the Genie was saying, somewhat oblivious to Aladdin's distress.

"What?" Aladdin looked up. "The Sultan just got done saying how honest and sincere I am."

"You're not getting any more honest and sincere sitting here," the Genie replied logically, and Aladdin groaned, his head dropping back into his hands.

"I'm going to tell her," he mumbled. "I just have to wait until the right time."

"Which is when, exactly?" the Genie pressed.

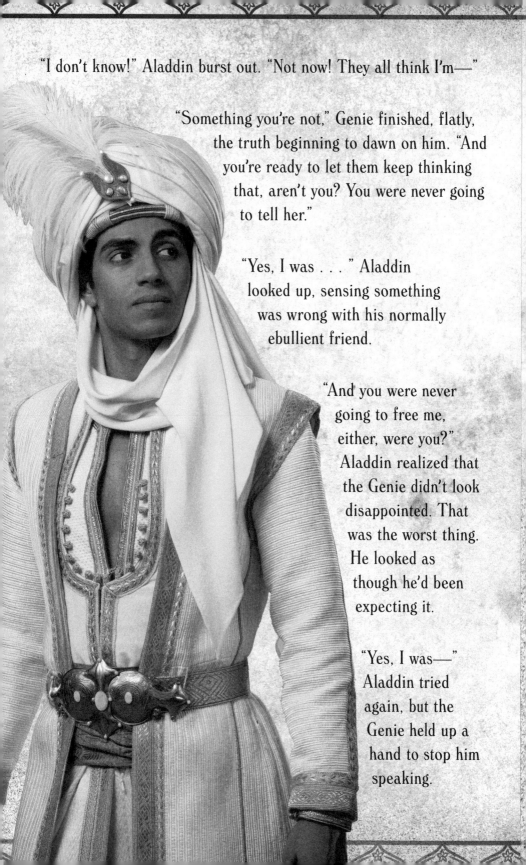

"I don't know!" Aladdin burst out. "Not now! They all think I'm—"

"Something you're not," Genie finished, flatly, the truth beginning to dawn on him. "And you're ready to let them keep thinking that, aren't you? You were never going to tell her."

"Yes, I was . . ." Aladdin looked up, sensing something was wrong with his normally ebullient friend.

"And you were never going to free me, either, were you?" Aladdin realized that the Genie didn't look disappointed. That was the worst thing. He looked as though he'd been expecting it.

"Yes, I was—" Aladdin tried again, but the Genie held up a hand to stop him speaking.

Then he seemed to reconsider. It wasn't worth it. The Genie retreated into the lamp, silently.

"Hey!" Aladdin yelled, after him, picking up the lamp and peering down at it. "I'm still talking to you!"

But there was no reply. Clearly the Genie had said all he wanted to say for now.

Aladdin stared, then shoved the lamp into his pocket. He needed to get out of the palace. Clear his head. He glared at Abu and the magic carpet, who had been silently watching the exchange. "Come on," he said, motioning for them to follow, but they both shrank back from him, nervous at his obvious anger.

"Fine!" Aladdin shouted to the air, throwing his hands up, as he stalked out. After a moment's hesitation, Abu followed. There was no telling what kind of trouble Aladdin would get into without him, after all.

Outside the palace, Abu perched on his shoulder, Aladdin couldn't help but replay Genie's words over and over in his head. He was becoming like Jafar? Impossible! He was nothing like Jafar. "Who does he think he is?" Aladdin demanded, glancing at Abu. "He's supposed to serve *me*, right?"

He was so furious with the Genie and with himself that he wasn't looking where he was going, and an old beggar stumbled into his path. "Hey, watch where you're going!" Aladdin snapped as they collided, the old man staggering backward. Aladdin stormed away from him without a word of apology, still fuming, complaining to Abu. "I haven't changed, have I?"

Abu gave him a carefully blank look, and Aladdin felt his anger begin to fade. The Genie had been right. He had changed, and for the worse.

Aladdin didn't think about where he was going. He'd wandered the streets of Agrabah for so long that his feet had a mind of their own, and they took him back to his old stomping grounds, the market, his hideaway. He looked around the trappings of his old life and realized that he couldn't just leave it behind. This is what had made him who he was—and he couldn't lie any longer.

"Genie was right," he said aloud. "I have to tell Jasmine the truth."

Unfortunately, this moment of poignant self-reflection came a little too late.

Unknown to Aladdin or the Sultan, Jafar had not fled far from the palace. Like Aladdin, he'd once been a street rat on these very streets, and he knew exactly how and where to lay low. With what magic remained to him, he had disguised himself . . . as an old beggar. And he waited.

~

Lindy: Oh no . . .

The Mariner: I am afraid so.

~

It had been the work of a moment to lift the lamp from Aladdin's pocket when they "accidentally" collided. The boy had not even noticed its absence. Now, standing in a dark alleyway just outside of the palace, Jafar at last had everything he wanted in the palm of his hand.

He rubbed the lamp.

"You had better be ready to apologize," the Genie began, then stopped short as he realized just who was holding the lamp this time. Not who he had been expecting. And yet, not unexpected. He sighed deeply at Jafar's haughty, expectant gaze, and began again.

"Oh great one who summons me and terrible one who commands me. . ."

"You're allergic to being happy, that's your problem," Dalia told Jasmine, watching her friend and princess stroke Raja sadly. She had watched her friend struggle with her decision about Ali for several hours now.

"I know," Jasmine replied. "I know that Ali is wonderful and I should just marry him and forget that my father doesn't think that I am fit to be Sultan, but I just . . . can't. I can't settle for only that."

She was about to say more, but the sound of the guards raising the alarm interrupted her before she could complete her thought. As the shouts became clearer, so did the reason for the panic. Jafar was in the palace. Jasmine leapt to her feet, sprinting toward the throne room. She arrived just behind her father, Dalia at her heels, eyes wide.

There on the throne, lounging as though he belonged there, was Jafar.

"Arrest him!" the Sultan was shouting, and the guards were closing in, but Jafar lifted his hand, holding aloft the lamp. It was as if time itself stopped. The Genie emerged from the lamp, and Jasmine and Dalia recognized him—Prince Ali's advisor.

"Sorry," the Genie whispered to Dalia, shamefaced. "I work for him now." He motioned to Jafar, and Dalia looked stunned, then disappointed as realization dawned.

"Genie," Jafar announced broadly, "I am ready to make my first wish. I wish to be Sultan of Agrabah."

"What?!" demanded the Sultan, but the Genie was already bowing. "Your wish is my command," he said, sadly.

Thunder crashed and lightning arced across the sky outside. Standing among the tatters of his old life, Aladdin looked up in alarm as an all-too-familiar haze of blue smoke began billowing up around the palace. Reflexively his hand went to his pocket.

No lamp.

Aladdin immediately realized what had happened and cursed his prideful foolishness. There was no time to feel sorry for himself—he knew what this meant. Jafar had the lamp, and Aladdin had a very short time to get to the palace to rescue everyone from the danger he'd put them all in. He broke into a run and headed straight for the palace.

Royalty and servants alike looked on aghast as Jafar stood before them, transformed, wearing the robes of the Sultan. Even the palace around them had shifted menacingly.

Jafar examined his new royal attire with immense satisfaction, then nodded to Hakim, the head of the guard. "My first act as Sultan!" he said to the guard. "Marshal an army! We march on Shirabad."

"You can't do that!" Jasmine shouted. Shirabad—her mother's home. It was unthinkable.

Jafar sneered. He no longer had to pretend to be polite. "I think we've all heard quite enough from you. Princesses should be pretty and silent." He made a dismissive gesture. "Guards, remove her!" Hakim hesitated, then signaled to his guards, who seized Jasmine. Jasmine fought back with all her strength.

"Jasmine, don't provoke him," the Sultan begged.

Jasmine balled her hands into fists. She loved her father, but she would not obey. She would not be silent. She would never accept this. Defiant, she broke away from the guards who tried to hold her back, striding back into the throne room. She ignored Jafar, passed him, and walked instead to Hakim. She gazed up at him steadily, knowingly, as she addressed him.

"Hakim, you are our most trusted soldier," she said. "I know you to be both loyal and just. But you must choose, now. Duty isn't always honor. Jafar may claim the title of Sultan, but he is not worthy of your admiration or your sacrifice. You know he seeks glory for himself, not Agrabah. Will you follow the man who wishes to destroy our beloved kingdom, or will you stand with me against him?"

The world seemed to hold its breath. Hakim hesitated.

Then he stepped closer to Jasmine, offering her a reverent bow. "I stand with you, Princess," he said softly. "Always." He turned to confront Jafar. "Arrest him!" he barked to his guards, who moved to seize the pretender to the throne.

~

Lindy: yesss. I love this princess!

Jafar felt rage boiling up inside him. Even now he was being overridden, ignored, insulted. "I should have known," he said. "But no matter. If you won't bow before a Sultan . . . then you will cower before a sorcerer!"

He clutched the lamp, looking toward the Genie. "Genie! I wish to become the most powerful sorcerer in the world!"

Aladdin, with the help of the magic carpet, had arrived outside the throne room just in time to hear Jafar's second wish. Gesturing for the

carpet to stay hidden, he crept forward, watching as Genie was forced to work his magic. There was a magical explosion, smoke swirling around Jafar and obscuring his form until he stepped forward, in elaborate robes and holding a new magic staff, larger and more ornate than the one that Aladdin had broken hours before.

Perhaps Aladdin gasped, or perhaps Jafar's new powers gave him superior senses—either way, he spotted Aladdin and Abu lurking in the shadows and chuckled. "Well, well. If it isn't Prince Ali."

He gestured with his new staff, and Aladdin was dragged forward, made helpless by Jafar's sorcery. He was unable to speak, or to move as Jafar changed his princely finery to the same ragged clothing he'd been wearing when he met Jasmine in the marketplace. Jafar had undone his wish—no more Prince Ali.

"You're actually—" Jasmine gasped. "You mean you weren't a prince that was pretending to be a commoner in the marketplace?"

"I can explain," Aladdin began, but Jafar cut him off.

"He's been pretending the entire time, Princess. He is an imposter." He strolled toward Aladdin, his voice filled with contempt. "Even with the power of the lamp, you couldn't wish yourself worthy. You're an insignificant irritation, and one I no longer need to tolerate."

Aladdin hung his head. Of all the ways for Jasmine to find out the truth . . .

But that was the least of his worries at the moment.

Jafar had finished humiliating him—and he had a good idea of how to deal with Aladdin once and for all. He raised his staff. "I think that banishment to the ends of the earth is a fitting punishment for all the trouble you've caused me," he said, with satisfaction.

Aladdin felt magic surround him and Abu, and before he could even draw his next breath, the throne room vanished, replaced by a sheet of white.

The cold hit him next, horrible, numbing cold that instantly froze him down to his bones. He fell to his knees and below him was white . . . snow? He'd heard of it, but never seen it with his own eyes. He cast about in desperation, but there was nothing but swirling white all around him, a vast snowfield as far as he could see. Wherever Jafar had sent him, he was a long, long way from Agrabah.

Aladdin watched his breath crystallize in the air and knew that if he stayed where he was, he wouldn't last much longer. He forced himself to his feet, staggering forward through the blizzard.

~

Barro: What about Abu?

The Mariner: Patience, we'll get to that.

~

In the throne room, Jafar turned his attention back to the Sultan and Jasmine. Behind him, the Genie signaled to the magic carpet, who he'd spotted still cowering behind a pillar. He knew where Jafar had banished Aladdin, and whispered a destination into the carpet's tassels. As he watched his old friend fly off, unseen by anyone but him, the Genie hoped it wasn't too little, too late.

Aladdin's teeth chattered as he trudged through the snow, realizing that he'd lost all feeling in his fingers and toes. Then, atop a drift of ice, he spotted a small, dark figure. He hurried forward, recognizing the form of Abu.

~

Barro: Thank goodness! You scared me, Baba!

The Mariner: Come on, I'd never let anything happen to that monkey.

~

Aladdin fought through the wind and cold to his friend's side. Abu was alive, but shivering, and Aladdin tucked him into his vest, huddling with him in a vain attempt to keep both of them warm. "I'm sorry, buddy," he said, sorrow in his voice. "This is all my fault." He knew that he should have freed the Genie when he had the chance. If he had, then Jafar would never have been able to wreak such havoc on Agrabah.

Aladdin lifted his head to start walking again—only to see a familiar rectangular shape descending from the sky.

"I've never been so happy to see a rug in my life," he said to the carpet as the enchanted object floated closer, allowing them to climb aboard. "Come on. We have to get back to Agrabah and fix what I did."

Carpet took off, sailing back through the air toward home.

Jafar might have been done with Aladdin, but he had considerable unfinished business with the Sultan. Now that he had taken his rightful place, he would never let the Sultan forget it.

Still, he craved more. Simply ruling Agrabah, or leading a conquering army to the neighboring kingdoms, these were not enough for Jafar. He would take away what the Sultan loved most. He would marry Princess Jasmine.

He presented this plan as fact. Jasmine refused at first, but eventually agreed after Jafar threatened to harm her father. After all, she'd already seen what he'd done to Aladdin.

But now he was standing in front of her, their wedding underway. Everything, Jafar thought, was perfect.

That is, until Aladdin came swooping in atop the magic carpet.

He dove at Jafar, knocking him backward and off-balance. The lamp, tied at his waist, was exposed and visible for a few crucial seconds, and Jasmine leapt forward and grabbed it.

"Here!" Aladdin called, holding his hand out to her, and Jasmine leapt aboard Carpet. The two of them raced away from the palace, the lamp clutched in Jasmine's hand.

Jasmine, alone with Aladdin as they sailed through the sky, was finally able to ask him the question that had been burning inside her. "Why did you lie to me?"

"I wanted to be worthy of you," Aladdin replied.

Jasmine made a disgusted sound. "By lying?"

Any further conversation was cut off by the sudden appearance of a pursuer in the skies behind them. It was Iago, but terrifyingly transformed by Jafar's sorcery. The little parrot was a now a fiery phoenix, so large that it left a trail like a comet as it chased them through the air above Agrabah.

Aladdin knew they wouldn't win in the open. Time to return to the place he knew best. He guided Carpet down toward the streets, hoping to lose Iago in the alleyways.

As they swooped low, however, the phoenix dived at the carpet, and the lamp fell from Jasmine's hands and toward the marketplace below, where it landed on the table of a lamp seller.

Abu jumped down to fetch it, only to find himself staring at dozens of identical lamps. He grabbed one at random, tossing it back up to Jasmine and Aladdin, who were forced to dodge away as the raging phoenix dove at them again.

"What do we do now?" Jasmine asked.

"If we go back to the palace, he'll kill us." Aladdin rubbed his chin, trying desperately to think of some way, any way, to fix the mess he had caused. Jafar had demonstrated his new power, and Aladdin was not eager to face him again. Not without a plan.

"My father is in there," Jasmine said, looking back toward the palace.

"And my friend," said Aladdin, following her gaze and thinking of the Genie. If only he'd listened to his friend when he had the chance. "But Jafar has the lamp. And he won't stop with Agrabah. He won't ever stop, nothing will ever be enough . . ."

Aladdin froze, remembering Genie's words to him. "I know what to do," he said, suddenly.

He had a plan. A crazy plan, but one that still might work. He looked to Carpet, who was still slowly unravelling from the lightning strike, looking shabbier and shabbier by the moment. "Can you help us get back inside the palace, buddy?" Despite everything, Carpet nodded his tassels.

~

Jafar caressed the lamp, back in his hands once more. Everything was as it should be. He was the ruler of Agrabah, and the world's most powerful sorcerer. And he still had one wish remaining. Nothing could stop him. Perhaps Aladdin and the princess had escaped, but he had all the time in the world to track them down again. And even if he never saw them again . . .

That thought was interrupted as Jasmine and Aladdin burst into the throne room, looking tattered from their recent battles, and—never one to waste an opportunity—Jafar raised his staff to strike them down.

"You've made this easy for me," he said, chuckling. "I would have let you live, but now . . . " He gathered his power. "You will die."

Aladdin stood still, however, not hiding and meeting Jafar's eyes, undaunted. "I'm not afraid of you," he said, calmly.

"You should be," Jafar snapped back, hurling a bolt of magic toward Aladdin.

Aladdin dodged, the bolt barely missing and taking a sizeable chunk out of the wall behind him. He tried to remain calm. He had to sell it—his plan wouldn't work otherwise. "Why?" he said, his tone mocking. "You think you're so powerful—"

"I am the most powerful sorcerer there is!" Jafar bellowed. He aimed another magical strike at Aladdin's head, missed again as Aladdin leapt nimbly to one side.

"If you were the most powerful, you wouldn't need the lamp." Aladdin's voice was a taunt, even as he struggled to keep his hands from shaking. "You're nothing without the Genie. He's the one who gave you your power, which means that he's much more powerful than you."

Jafar, about to aim another bolt of magic, hesitated, Aladdin's words ringing true. Genie watched in horror as Aladdin continued, "Face it Jafar, you're still only the second most powerful man in the room. And that means you're nothing."

Jafar lowered his staff, frowning, eyeing Aladdin, considering, then whirled to face the Genie.

"My final wish . . . " Jafar snarled. "Genie! I wish to be the most powerful being in the world. Even more powerful than you!"

~

Barro: Is he crazy?

Lindy: Ohhhh! I get it!

Barro: What? What did you get?

The Genie had at first been horrified when Aladdin began goading Jafar—but now he saw that his friend had left him a glorious loophole.

"Most powerful," Genie repeated. "Are you sure . . . ?"

"Do it!" Jafar roared.

The Genie shrugged. "Most powerful being in the world, coming right up."

He motioned his hands, and everyone in the room held their breath once more as that familiar blue smoke surrounded Jafar, who began to transform . . . into an enormous red Genie.

"I feel it!" Jafar crowed as his body and his powers grew. "I feel the power of the cosmos coursing through my veins! I am unstoppable!" Infinite magic at his fingertips . . . but as he tried to use it, nothing happened. He tried again. Nothing.

"Forget something?" came Aladdin's voice at his feet. Jafar glared down at Aladdin, who smiled back up at him beatifically.

"A Genie without a master has one problem," Aladdin continued, nodding to Genie. "Phenomenal cosmic power . . ."

With satisfaction, Genie snapped his fingers, summoning a tiny lamp.

"Itty-bitty living space."

Jafar tried to pull away as his new lamp tried to pull him in, grabbing for something, anything, trying in vain to use the powers he'd been granted—but all he managed was to grab Iago, who was sucked into the confines of the lamp with him, vanishing.

Aladdin picked up the lamp, then handed it to the Genie. Genie grinned, then sent the lamp rocketing away into the distance like a firework. "A couple thousand years in The Cave of Wonders ought to cool him off!" he said, with satisfaction.

Aladdin looked up to see the Sultan and Jasmine walking toward him. "How can we ever thank you?" the Sultan asked, but Aladdin stopped him.

"Don't thank me. But please, accept my apology. I'm sorry that I lied to you both." He turned to Jasmine. "Especially you. You deserve so much more."

"We all make mistakes, my boy," said the Sultan, comfortingly, then looked at Jasmine as well. "Even Sultans. It was my mistake to trust Jafar, and my mistake to underestimate you, my beloved daughter. You have the courage of a leader, I see that now. No ancient rules can change that." He took Jasmine's hand as she looked at him in amazement. "You will be the next Sultan, and rule over Agrabah. No marriage . . . no prince . . . required."

Tears sprang to Jasmine's eyes as her father finally saw her for who she truly was. She nodded, gratefully. "Thank you, Baba," she whispered. It was all she had ever wanted.

She looked to where Aladdin stood a distance away, watching them.

. . . Almost all.

"Don't worry," Genie whispered to Aladdin. "You still have one wish left. Boom, we make you a prince again and this time there's no Jafar to undo it. You can still get the girl."

"Can you really do that?" Aladdin asked, still gazing at Jasmine.

Genie nodded, putting his lamp back in Aladdin's hands. "Just gotta say the words, kid. I wish . . ."

Aladdin took a deep breath.

"I wish . . . to set you free, Genie."

"As you wi . . . wait, what?" Genie stopped, then shook his head, peering closer at Aladdin. "What did you say?" He wasn't sure he had heard correctly.

But Aladdin didn't have to say anything else. He just smiled as the familiar magic smoke surrounded his friend. Genie could feel his own magic draining away—but a wonderful sense of freedom taking its place. He was no longer a magical being of infinite cosmic energy. He was just a mortal man.

And it felt wonderful.

"Quick," he said to Aladdin. "Ask me to do something."

"Get me an apple," Aladdin suggested.

"Get it yourself!" the Genie shouted, then burst out laughing, overjoyed. He had never expected this. He had hoped, he had dreamed . . . but his wish had finally come true.

"What's next?" Aladdin asked, watching the Genie's expression. His friend's obvious delight made him smile, but there was a little sadness, too—wherever the Genie went next, it would be without him.

The Genie stared up at the sky, suddenly overwhelmed by all the possibilities. "I don't know for sure," he admitted, then gave a sly smile. "But there is a certain handmaid that I really, really like. I might start by asking her for another date . . ."

He paused, then hugged Aladdin tightly. After all he'd been through, with all he had at stake, Aladdin had still kept his promise. It was something the Genie would never forget. "Thank you, . . . my friend," he said, and Aladdin grinned in return, knowing how much it meant to have the Genie call him "friend" at last.

Released from the Genie's bear hug, Aladdin looked around. Jafar was defeated. The Genie was free. Jasmine was going to become the next Sultan. Not bad, for a street rat, he thought. He turned to scoop up Abu. "C'mon buddy," he said softly. "Let's go home."

He walked out of the palace, taking one last look at his surroundings as he passed through the enormous palace gates. He reached into his pocket, and pulled out Jasmine's hairpin—the half he had taken that day they'd first met, when he snuck into the palace, still thinking she was a handmaid. He sighed. It had been fun while it lasted.

"Stop!" came a familiar voice from behind him. Aladdin spun around to see Jasmine running after him, smiling as she caught up to him.

"Am I in trouble?" Aladdin smiled back.

"Only because you got caught." Jasmine retorted, and took out her half of the hairpin. She walked up to him, pinning the two pieces together, then pulled Aladdin toward her to kiss him.

When she came up for breath, she said, "You know, now that I'm Sultan, I can marry whoever I want."

"Is that so?" asked Aladdin, grinning dreamily, and hand-in-hand, they walked back through the palace gates.

~

The Mariner: The end.

Lindy: What? "The end??"

Lindy: You can't end the story there, Baba!

Barro: Where did the Genie go?

Lindy: Did Princess Jasmine and Aladdin get married?

Barro: What happened to the monkey?!

The Mariner: Well . . .

Lindy: Well??

The Mariner: Well, I can tell you what happened to the Genie. He and his beloved Dalia went off to see the world together. They found a sailing ship, and although it was old, and a little rickety, it served them well through many storms.

Lindy: No way.

Barro: What?

The Mariner: They saw many beautiful sights, and met many wonderful people, and the Genie was happier than he had ever been in his life. Especially when Dalia bore him two wonderful, if slightly meddlesome, children . . .

Barro: No way.

The Mariner: . . . named Lindy and Barro . . .

Lindy: Baba!

The Mariner: Look to the city on the horizon, my children. We are nearly there. Does anyone want to guess what city that is?

Barro: No way . . .

Lindy: It can't be . . .

The Mariner: Oh, but it is. Agrabah!

~

Lindy and Barro watched as the city came into view. As their father drew the boat alongside the docks, they saw a golden carriage approach.

The Genie took his wife Dalia's hand, disembarking from his ship, his children following close at his heels. He smiled as the the carriage doors opened, and two regal figures emerged, to cries of delight from his children. They could only be Aladdin and Jasmine from the story their father had just told—both of them dressed in fine clothing.

"Are you the princess?" Lindy asked, eagerly, and her mother nudged her.

"Actually, she's Sultan now," Dalia said, with a gentle smile.

"It's good to see you, my friend," Aladdin said, embracing the Genie. "Agrabah hasn't been the same without you. I hope your arrival means you're considering our offer."

"What offer, Baba?" Barro asked, eyes wide as he looked to his father.

"To live here with us," said Jasmine. "In the palace."

"I'm not the one you have to convince." Genie gazed down at his children, fondly. "What do you say, kids?" he asked, as the magic carpet descended from the sky. His kids fairly screamed with excitement, hugging their father and jumping up and down. "That might be a 'yes,'" he admitted.

"But it's not fair, Baba!" said Lindy, suddenly, looking up at her father. "You did so much for everyone else, and never got any wishes of your own."

"Oh, now that's not true," said the Genie, hugging them tightly, and looking up at Dalia with love in his eyes. "I have everything I've ever wanted right here."

Studio Fun International

An imprint of Printers Row Publishing Group

A division of Readerlink Distribution Services, LLC

10350 Barnes Canyon Road, Suite 100, San Diego, CA 92121

www.studiofun.com

Written by: Rachael Upton

Illustrated by: Luigi Aimè

Designed by: Tiffany Meador-LaFleur

Printers Row Publishing Group is a division of Readerlink Distribution Services, LLC.
Studio Fun International is a registered trademark of Readerlink Distribution Services, LLC.
All notations of errors or omissions should be addressed to Studio Fun International, Editorial
Department, at the above address.

ISBN: 978-0-7944-4232-3

Manufactured, printed and assembled in Stevens Point, Wisconsin, USA
First printing, March 2019. WOR/03/19
23 22 21 20 19 1 2 3 4 5